THEWIZARDCOW

The Dream Eater's Grin

A Journey Through A Mind of Nightmares

Contents

1

Chapter 1: The Ultimatum

The overhead lights buzzed with a dull, electric hum as the protagonist—Cyran—stood in the center of the interrogation room, wrists cuffed to a metal table that stank of disinfectant. The white walls were too bright, too clean, as if desperate to erase the memory of what this place truly was: a holding pen for disgraced Dreamweavers and a corridor leading to death sentences. The government's Dream Department had a penchant for oppressive sterility. There were no windows. The only furniture—a table, two chairs, and a monitoring device wired into the walls— seemed reduced to skeletal essentials. It was as if the room had been bleached not just of color, but of mercy.

Cyran could feel the presence of guards behind the one-way observation window. They were little more than silhouettes in their memory, but the scrape of boots, the low murmurs, the occasional hiss of a radio transmission reached through the soundproofing somehow. They knew the watchers were anxious. Everyone was. What was about to happen here had no precedent that ended well.

The door hissed open, and a figure stepped inside: a woman, tall and severe, with silver hair braided down her spine. She wore the dark navy coat of the Department's upper echelons. No name tag. The only adornment on her coat was a slender badge in the shape of an eye, indicating her clearance—top level.

Her presence seemed to drain the oxygen from the room.

Cyran's heart kicked. They'd been waiting for hours, imagining what this meeting would bring. Punishment? A chance? They'd heard rumors on the block, stories whispered by other Dreamweavers who had fallen out of favor: The Department sometimes offered impossible deals to those with nothing left to lose. The last time they tried something like that had been with the Dream Eater's mind...and everyone knew how that ended.

"Cyran," the woman said, voice crisp. She took a seat opposite without waiting for an invitation. Her gloved fingers drummed once, twice on the metal. She gave no hint of emotion, only a meticulous calm, like a surgeon preparing an incision. "I trust you're well enough to have a conversation."

The cuffs chafed Cyran's wrists. They nodded stiffly. Their voice came out hoarse when they spoke. "As well as can be expected, given the circumstances."

A flicker of something—maybe approval at their composure, or simple acknowledgment—crossed her angular face. "Let's dispense with pleasantries. Your record: once commendable, now tarnished. You failed in a high-profile case. The patient suffered irreversible neural damage. The Department does not forget such things."

Cyran swallowed. They remembered that case all too well. A man, a senator's son, plagued by nightmares so volatile that even experienced Dreamweavers struggled. Cyran had gone in hoping to prove themselves. They'd emerged with screams echoing in their mind and the senator's son left in a vegetative state. It didn't matter that the trauma had been severe. Failure in this line of work carried a heavy cost.

"Your expertise is still of interest to us," the woman continued. "We have a situation. You are aware of the prisoner known as the Dream Eater?"

A chill that had nothing to do with the room's sterile temperature crawled up Cyran's spine. The Dream Eater. The serial killer who had turned Dreamweaver after Dreamweaver into a twitching husk. The one responsible for the mass slaughter of their kind. Almost all of the best had tried to enter his mind to diagnose the root of his psychopathy. Every single one had died inside that labyrinth, their brains liquefied by horrors that no one could articulate.

"I'm aware," Cyran said, voice carefully steady.

"Good. Then you understand the gravity of what I'm about to say." The woman leaned forward. Her gray eyes were like chips of flint. "We need one final attempt at understanding him. He's contained—physically, at least—and sedated. But the killings have...changed things. We must know what truly happened inside his mind. Whether this madness can spread. Whether something else lurks within him. We want a full diagnostic."

Cyran's heart pounded. They'd spent the last few months expecting a quiet termination. Any disgraced Dreamweaver was a liability. Instead, here was an offer—no, a command. "You're asking me to go into his mind?" They tried to keep their voice from cracking. "No one's survived that."

"Not yet," she said, as if survival were a technicality. "You are expendable— let's be clear on that. We aren't offering absolution. If you refuse, you'll simply be decommissioned. If you accept and die inside his mind, it's no great loss from our perspective. But should you survive, should you bring back something useful, we might consider adjusting your record. Perhaps even reinstatement."

A suffocating silence followed. Cyran felt trapped. "You want me to go in and diagnose him. To...heal him?"

She didn't laugh, but the slightest tilt of her head conveyed cynicism. "Not necessarily heal. Understand. We want to know what he is. Whether the rumors of something else inside him—some presence that made him what he is—hold any truth. You've heard the stories. The others who went in babbled about a tall figure, grinning. Some called it a demon, some a manifestation of pure trauma. If it's just madness, fine. If it's something else, we need to know. And you, Cyran, will be our eyes."

Cyran tried not to show panic. "And if I say no?"

"Then this conversation ends, and your life as a Dreamweaver—and as anything else—ends shortly thereafter."

A bitter taste filled Cyran's mouth. They had nothing left. The Department's cold logic made the choice clear. Go in, die heroically or miraculously return. Or refuse, and be quietly executed. At least inside the Dream Eater's mind, there was the slimmest chance. A terrible, gut-wrenching chance, but a chance nonetheless.

They tried to straighten their posture. The cuffs rattled. "I'll do it."

"Very good." She stood, and as if on cue, the door swung open. A guard stepped in to unlock Cyran's cuffs. "You'll be prepped immediately. We have notes from previous attempts—though they're mostly useless. Still, perhaps they might give you a clue." Her gaze slid over Cyran's face, calculating. "Your equipment will be basic: a neural tether and a sedation link. We can't risk more elaborate measures. The Dream Eater's mind is...volatile."

Cyran rubbed their wrists as soon as they were free. Needles of pain pricked under the skin, but freedom of movement felt like a small victory. "What do I need to know?"

A faint smirk touched the corner of her lips. "I suggest you remember your training. Distinguish your own psyche from his illusions. His mind is known to prey on weaknesses. If there's anything in your past you haven't reconciled, it will come back twisted and hungry. Be prepared."

Cyran's chest tightened at the memory of their last failed patient. That scene would doubtless return, sick and contorted. "Understood," they managed.

"Then follow the guards. They'll take you to the prep room. You go in within the hour."

As the guards shepherded Cyran into the corridor, the woman's words lingered. The corridor was as white and sparse as the interrogation room— these halls were built to break the human spirit, or so it seemed. Sterile to the point of madness.

They passed a window. Through reinforced glass, Cyran glimpsed the Dream Eater's cell. The figure lay strapped to a bed—barely human-looking under thick restraints and breathing apparatus. Even from a distance, something about the shape of his body seemed off. His limbs were too still, too rigid, as if posed. The skin on his face was pale, almost translucent under the harsh lights. His eyes were open, unblinking, staring at nothing. Yet, for a second, Cyran felt like they made eye contact. A shiver crawled down their spine. What did the killer dream about when all external stimuli were cut off? Did the grinning entity lounge in the darkness of his mind, waiting?

They thought of the stories. Dreamweavers who tried and failed. Some woke screaming, blood pouring from their noses and ears, talking about a grin that moved like a living thing. Others never woke at all.

A sudden squeal of static crackled over a distant intercom. Cyran's escort tensed, pressing a hand to an earpiece. The sound cut off as abruptly as it began. The guard at their left—a younger man with hollow eyes—whispered under his breath: "It's this place. He messes with the systems." His partner glared at him, and he fell silent.

Eventually, they reached a small room lined with advanced medical equipment. A technician awaited them: a slender older man with thinning hair and an unsmiling mouth. He nodded curtly and motioned to a reclining chair connected to a nest of wires and tubes.

"Sit," he said. "We'll run a quick neurological baseline. Then sedation and insertion."

Cyran obeyed, heart thumping. They leaned back, and the cold synthetic leather of the chair squeaked under their weight. Electrodes were pasted onto their temples, chest, and the back of their neck. The technician adjusted a series of dials and studied monitors that spat out lines of neon-green data.

As they worked, Cyran's mind drifted. They recalled the old training halls where Dreamweavers learned to navigate psyches: simple exercises in calm, controlled mental landscapes. Nothing like the tempest of madness inside the Dream Eater. The mentors had warned them that some minds were beyond help, beyond understanding. What if this was one of those minds? But there was no turning back.

"Baseline stable," the technician said quietly. He turned a valve on a small silver canister, releasing a hissing puff of gas into the room's filtration system. "Count backward from ten."

Cyran inhaled. A slow numbness crept through their veins. "Ten... nine... eight..." Their voice thickened. They felt their limbs grow distant, heavy. A dim haze gathered at the edges of their vision. "Seven... s-six..."

The room blurred, and reality began to tilt. The last thing they saw before the darkness took them was the observation window. Behind it stood the silver-haired woman, arms folded, eyes unreadable. Something caught the light—a reflection in the glass. Was it just a distortion, or something tall and thin, grinning in the background?

Cyran awoke, or at least they thought they did, in a dim corridor that smelled of wet earth and rusted metal. The transition from sedation chamber to here had been instantaneous. One moment drifting off, the next jolting awake in a shadowy hallway. The temperature felt unnaturally cool. Bare bulbs swung overhead, their filaments buzzing. A feeling of wrongness pervaded the air, a sense that this place was alive and aware of them.

They took a tentative step. The floorboards groaned as if they were bones bending under weight. On the walls, portraits in ornate frames stared down. Each painting was a portrait of a face in mid-scream, but each scream was pulled into a wide, mocking grin. It was as if the mouths had been stretched by invisible hooks.

"Stay calm," Cyran muttered. They reached into their mental toolkit—techniques for stabilizing their sense of self inside a foreign psyche. Identify anchor points: Name: Cyran. Occupation: Dreamweaver. Goal: Diagnose the Dream Eater. Physical form: Humanoid. They repeated these facts in their mind, weaving a mental cocoon of identity.

A faint laugh drifted down the corridor. It didn't sound like any single human voice, more like a chorus of whispers forming a laugh-shaped sound. Cyran felt the hairs on their neck rise. The corridor stretched into darkness, and with no alternative, they followed it.

As they moved deeper, the corridor's floor buckled and changed. The wood planks underfoot warped into something like flesh, then back to wood again in a nauseating cycle. Their breath sounded too loud in their ears. At the end of the corridor stood a mirror—tarnished, edges flecked with mold. In its surface, Cyran saw their own reflection: exhausted, eyes ringed with shadows. But behind them, towering in the darkness, a shape elongated and bent over their shoulder. Before Cyran could turn around, the light flickered and the shape vanished.

Just an illusion? Or was it here too?

They pressed forward, pushing through a door at the corridor's end. It opened into a small chamber cluttered with debris. Torn scraps of cloth, shards of glass, and twisted metal littered the floor. In the center lay something that made Cyran's stomach clench: the body of a Dreamweaver—or what was left of it. The body had been arranged in a macabre puzzle, pieces disassembled and then reassembled wrongly. The head was placed too far from the shoulders, the arms twisted back at impossible angles. Yet the corpse's face bore a cracked grin, lips split from stretching too wide.

Cyran's heart pounded. This must be the fate of one who came before. A reminder. They turned their gaze away, focusing instead on the subtle differences in air pressure, in the textures of sound. They needed clues, something to lead them deeper, to understand the pathology before madness took hold.

A voice, barely audible, skittered along the chamber's walls: "He showed me the grin... now I see truth..." The words warped into laughter and died away. Cyran shuddered. They needed to find a foothold in this place. Perhaps other rooms would hold scraps of memory. The Dream Eater's reason for murdering Dreamweavers had to be here, encoded in these nightmares.

As they exited the chamber, they felt the presence again—just outside their field of vision. It was as if the entity hovered at the edges, stepping forward only when not observed. The faint smell of rotting leaves and dust swirled in the air.

Cyran whispered an old mantra from training: "This is not my fear. This is not my weakness." But it sounded hollow here.

In the silence that followed, a quiet, echoing laughter responded, as if amused by their courage—or mocking it. And that grin, always that grin, lingered in the periphery of their mind's eye. It seemed to be waiting patiently for the next scene to unfold, and for Cyran to find themselves even more hopelessly entangled in the Dream Eater's horrors.

2

Chapter 2: Preparations & Warnings

Cyran moved through the dreamscape with measured steps, trying to keep their breathing steady. Every inch of this place radiated a malevolent intelligence. They had started in a corridor of shifting wooden floors and unnerving portraits. Now, after discovering the mangled remains of a previous Dreamweaver, they found themselves at a branching point: the corridor split into multiple passages, each poorly lit and twisting into shadowed uncertainty.

They paused, heart still thudding, and tried to recall their training. Before entering a subject's mind, Dreamweavers learned to build mental "anchors," cognitive constructs designed to stabilize one's sense of self. But this place felt corrosive to those standard techniques—like acid slowly dissolving the mental ropes Cyran had prepared. Still, they had to try.

They closed their eyes, drawing inward. "My name is Cyran," they thought firmly, letting the words resound. "I was sent here to diagnose the Dream Eater. I am a visitor. I am not part of this mind." They shaped these affirmations into a mental shield. For a moment, the oppressive atmosphere lightened a fraction. A faint phosphorescent glow, perhaps a trick of their own psychic defenses, shimmered in their periphery. It was fragile, but it was something.

When they opened their eyes, they spotted a pale glimmer at the far end of one corridor. The other two corridors seemed darker, more claustrophobic, as if they tapered into fleshy tunnels. Considering their lack of bearings, Cyran headed toward the light. Each step echoed strangely, as though stepping in a cavern with a distant drip. The laughter that had haunted the previous hallway receded, replaced by a hush pregnant with anticipation.

Soon they emerged into a space that looked like a distorted version of a mentor's office—a memory from Cyran's own past, co-opted by the Dream Eater's mind. The furnishings were familiar yet wrong: a desk too tall and narrow, shelves holding books that bled ink, and a large anatomical chart of a human brain that changed each time they looked at it, adding or removing lobes, twisting neural pathways into impossible knots. It reminded Cyran that their own mind wasn't safe here either. The Dream Eater's psyche could pull from their subconscious, twisting it into cruel tableau.

A figure stood behind the desk. At first glance, it resembled one of Cyran's old mentors, Aurelius—a stoic man who'd once praised Cyran's potential. But as soon as the figure turned, Cyran saw the mentor's eyes were mismatched: one human, the other an empty black hole. His mouth twitched in a half-smile that tugged the corners far too wide.

"Cyran," the figure said, voice a perfect imitation of Aurelius's baritone. "I warned you against carelessness, didn't I?" The tone was conversational, yet laced with a cruel amusement. "You were always so desperate to prove yourself."

Cyran's hands curled into fists. They knew the rules: do not engage illusions as if they are real. They are fragments, pieces of trauma or predation within the mind. "You're not Aurelius," they said, careful to keep their voice steady. "You're just a manifestation of this place."

The figure's grin widened. "So assured." The desk between them groaned as if made from living wood. "Tell me, have you found what you're looking for? The truth behind the Dream Eater's madness? Or have you realized you'll share the fate of your predecessors?"

Behind the figure, the ink from the shelves' books dripped onto the floor, forming dark puddles that slowly shaped themselves into grinning faces. Cyran fought to ignore them. They needed information, not terror. "I know you're trying to unsettle me. It won't work."

"Does it not?" The fake Aurelius tilted its head. A wet sound, like flesh tearing, whispered through the room. "You failed once. What makes you think you can succeed here, in a mind that's already devoured better Dreamweavers than you?"

Cyran flinched at the reminder of their past failure. The entity seized on it, pressing closer. The grinning faces in the ink puddles began to mouth silent laughter.

"I'm not here to entertain you," Cyran said through gritted teeth. They drew a deep breath and summoned another mental anchor: a visualization of themselves standing on a high cliff under a clear sky. "I am here to do my job."

The figure's unnatural eye—the black void—narrowed, as if irritated. "Your job? Your job is to understand something beyond your comprehension." The voice lowered, grew harsher. "The Dream Eater saw the grin. He learned from it. He saw the truth behind dreams, behind the veil of sanity. And you—" it laughed softly, "you think you're safe because you have training?"

Cyran didn't answer. Instead, they stepped forward and reached for the desk. Their hand passed through it as if through mist, the entire scene flickering. An illusion. They were conversing with a mental defense, nothing more. Perhaps by pushing through, they could dissipate it.

A tremor shook the room. The figure hissed like steam escaping a pipe. The shelves rattled, and from the shaking books, black ink rained down, splattering on the floor and Cyran's boots. The ink was warm, alive, writhing across their feet. Cyran jerked back, disgusted.

Enough. They closed their eyes, focused on a technique learned in the Academy: Identify a focal point of the illusion and "overwrite" it with calm mental energy. They chose the figure's mismatched eyes. Concentrating, they visualized those eyes transforming into ordinary, inert marbles. They refused the logic of this twisted place. They forced normality upon it.

The figure snarled, and for an instant, the room flickered like a dying neon light. The desk warped, the books shrank, and then the entire scene collapsed into murky darkness. Cyran stumbled, arms out to catch their balance, and found themselves in a stark hallway again. Whether they had won a small victory or simply triggered the mind's reshuffling, they weren't sure.

The corridor ahead branched once more, this time into two paths: one sloping downward, the other leading to a door etched with strange glyphs. The glyphs resembled stylized smiles, arranged in patterns that made the eyes ache to look at.

Cyran considered their options. Downward likely led deeper, where the core of the Dream Eater's psyche might lurk. The door with the glyphs—could it represent a memory vault, a hidden aspect of the killer's past? They needed clues, something to help them understand the entity the Dream Eater had encountered or created.

With a steadying breath, they approached the etched door. The closer they got, the stronger a faint, foul smell became: decaying leaves and something chemical. A low chuckle seeped from beneath the door-frame. Cyran half-expected it to be locked, but when they touched the handle—a twisted piece of metal shaped like a grin—it gave easily. The door swung inward with a creak.

Beyond it lay a cramped room that looked like an archive of pain. The walls were plastered with newspaper clippings and photographs that constantly rearranged themselves. Cyran stepped inside, careful not to touch anything yet. As they watched, a photograph near their shoulder shimmered, showing a row of children's faces, all smiling for a school portrait. The image blurred, and the children's faces elongated into unsettling grins. Another clipping bore a headline—"DREAMWEAVER FOUND DEAD IN SUBCONSCIOUS SCENE"—and beneath it, smaller text that rearranged into nonsense symbols whenever Cyran tried to read it.

A table in the center held something tangible: a rolled-up scroll tied with what looked like a strip of skin. Cyran's stomach lurched, but they couldn't afford squeamishness. They reached out, carefully untying it and unrolling the parchment. Instead of ink, the letters seemed etched in charcoal and dried blood. They read:

"He whispered it to me in the dark. The grin behind all eyes. I saw it first in my reflection, then in theirs. I couldn't unsee it. I had to free them from the illusions they called dreams. They only saw the surface, never the truth. The grin, the grin, the grin..."

Cyran's eyes jumped over the words, hoping for something more concrete. Instead, they found only delirium and vague hints. "He whispered it to me"—who was he? The Dream Eater speaking of someone else or something else? Had this entity introduced a concept, a vision, that drove the killer to murder?

The scroll ended abruptly with a smear of black. Cyran dropped it back on the table, heart sinking. If this was the mind's attempt to give voice to the killer's inner thoughts, it lacked coherence. Still, it mentioned a reflection. That might be a clue—reflections often served as gateways or metaphors in dream interpretation. Perhaps the grin was first seen in some kind of mirror, or reflective surface. A trauma event where the Dream Eater saw something that forever changed him.

A whimpering sound drew Cyran's attention. They scanned the room, spotting a figure crouched in a corner, wrapped in heavy chains. The figure's outline was fuzzy, as if half-formed. It looked like a Dreamweaver—wearing the standard issue jumpsuit, electrodes embedded in the skull. Could this be the remnant of one of the earlier victims?

Cyran approached slowly, one hand raised in a placating gesture. "Can you hear me?" Their voice sounded alien in the stifling hush. "Are you real?"

The figure shuddered and lifted its head. Its face was a blurred smear, features shifting like paint in water. It spoke in a thin, reedy whisper: "You can't fight the grin. You can't reason with it. It's older than reason."

Cyran's throat tightened. "What is it? Is it just a hallucination, or something that made him—"

A rattling of chains as the figure jerked closer, face still indistinct. "We tried. We tried to excise it, to diagnose him as we do with any trauma. But this...this didn't respond. It saw us, too. It knew us. One by one, it took our minds. It fed on our fears and secrets, leaving behind only these twisted echoes. It told him—told the Dream Eater—lies or truths too big to hold." The voice broke, and the figure trembled, chains scraping on the floor.

Cyran fought a rising panic. If this was a memory-echo of a fallen Dreamweaver, it might hold valuable hints. "Listen to me," they said, forcing calm into their tone. "I need something actionable. How can I survive here?

How can I understand what caused this?"

The chained figure gave a soft, rasping laugh, like a knife on stone. "Survive? Understand? You're dealing with something that is not bound by the walls of this mind. Even now, it watches. Look—look at the walls!"

Cyran instinctively glanced at the walls. The clippings and photographs had shifted again. Now all showed variations of a single image: a tall, impossibly slender figure looming behind a child in a mirror's reflection. The child's face was terrified, the figure's grin grotesquely wide. In some images, the figure stood behind adults, behind victims, behind the Dream Eater himself. Always grinning, always present.

"What am I seeing?" Cyran whispered.

"An infection," the chained figure hissed. "A seed planted in the psyche, but it can sprout beyond the mind. You think dreams are private, but sometimes, something slips through. The Dream Eater was just... receptive. He let it in. He allowed the grin to guide him. And now—now we all suffer."

Cyran's spine prickled with cold dread. Was this entity a psychological parasite, or something worse? The Dream Eater's crimes suddenly seemed like symptoms, not the disease itself. Could the grin be spreading beyond dreams, influencing other minds? They thought of the asylum walls back in reality, the rumors and whispers from the guards.

They tried once more: "How do I stop it?"

The figure's blurred face twitched, a suggestion of eyes meeting Cyran's gaze. "I don't know if you can. But you must try to anchor yourself in reason. Remember who you are. Remember that you are here as an observer, a healer. You must find a core memory—an origin point—in the Dream Eater's mind. Something that predates the grin. If you can isolate that memory, you might reveal the truth. But beware—the grin will not let you do so easily."

Cyran stepped back, weighing these words. They were hardly reassuring, but it was direction. An origin point, something that showed the killer before the madness took root. "Thank you," they said quietly.

The figure's chains rattled, then began to dissolve, its entire form breaking apart into ash-like fragments. The last whisper drifted through the air: "It's watching us both right now..."

Alone again, Cyran turned to leave. The door was still open, and beyond it, the corridor pulsed with faint laughter. Before stepping out, they forced themselves to reassert their identity: "Cyran, Dreamweaver. I'm here to diagnose." They even recalled a bit of training advice from their old mentor Aurelius—the real Aurelius: *Always seek patterns. In the chaos of a tortured mind, patterns can lead you to the root.*

Patterns. The grin appeared in reflections, in distorted images, and was linked to the Dream Eater's awakening to some "truth." Perhaps the path downward—deeper into the labyrinth—would lead to earlier memories, maybe even childhood trauma. The grin might have first appeared there. Cyran would have to brave the deeper layers.

They stepped back into the corridor. The laughter was distant but insistent. The dreamscape felt more unstable now that Cyran had interacted with it on this level, as if the entity knew they were searching for origins. The floor rippled underfoot. Lights flickered overhead, and one of the corridor's walls bulged as if something massive pressed against it from the other side.

Cyran pressed on, choosing the downward path at the branching intersection. Each step seemed to lower them into a dimmer, more primal environment. The walls changed texture, from painted plaster to rough-hewn stone. The air grew damp and stale, like the depths of an old cellar. They could almost smell moss and old rot.

A faint whisper drifted through their mind—words they had read on the scroll: *He whispered it to me in the dark.* Perhaps that was where they were headed now: into the dark center of the Dream Eater's origin, where he first encountered the grin. Cyran braced themselves, determined to find at least some piece of clarity.

As they descended, the corridor widened, leading to a rough stone chamber. Its ceiling arched high, disappearing into shadow. Along the walls were carved faces—hundreds of them—each with that unnatural smile. The sight twisted Cyran's stomach, but they pushed forward. These carvings might be older, more fundamental memories. The Dream Eater's mind was assembling them here, perhaps as a barricade.

Halfway across the chamber, a deep, resonant laughter echoed from above.

Cyran froze, scanning the gloom. They caught a glimpse of movement in the darkness overhead—a long, spindly limb unfurling, as if belonging to a creature perched on the ceiling.

"Focus," they whispered to themselves. If they panicked, they'd lose the tenuous grip they held on their identity. They needed to keep going, find whatever core memory existed deeper inside. Yet the presence above was clearly no illusion of a friendly mentor, no mere fragment. This might be the entity itself.

They took one cautious step, then another, trying to reach the opposite archway that promised further descent. The laughter followed, thick and mocking, its sound resonating inside Cyran's skull rather than their ears.

Then, silence.

With a final, steadying breath, Cyran slipped through the archway and continued downward, determined not to look back. The grin's presence had been felt, acknowledged. Now they needed to learn its secrets and survive. In the process, maybe they would prove to the Department—and to themselves— that they were more than just a disgraced Dreamweaver. They would make sense of this madness, or be consumed by it.

At the bottom of the next slope, the dim light revealed another corridor—this one lined with doors, each door bearing a different reflection in its polished surface. In every reflection, Cyran saw that tall, thin shape lurking behind them. No matter how often they turned, there was nothing standing there. It was always just in the mirror, grinning with empty eyes.

They pressed on, heart pounding, guided by the faint hope that somewhere ahead lay a memory pure enough to reveal how it all began. And behind them, soundless yet certain, the grin followed.

3

Chapter 3: Into the Grinning Halls

Cyran advanced cautiously down the corridor of mirrored doors, each one a narrow rectangle of polished metal with ornate hinges. Their own reflection wavered on every surface, lit by no discernible source except a sickly phosphorescence that seemed to seep from the walls. The passage was unnaturally silent, save for the echo of their footsteps and the faint squeak of their boots on the damp floor. Yet, no matter how quietly they moved, their reflection always revealed that looming, elongated figure at their back. The grin drifted behind them like a malignant shadow, even though when Cyran glanced over a shoulder, the corridor remained empty.

"I am Cyran," they reminded themselves softly, voice turning to a whisper in this hush. "I'm a Dreamweaver, an observer, not part of this mind." Their mantra steadied them, if only a little.

As they passed each door, strange shapes flickered in the reflections. One door's surface showed them standing knee-deep in a swamp, black reeds and twisting vines coiled around their legs, though the corridor's floor remained solid stone. Another door's reflection flickered with images of children laughing in a playground—until all at once, the children turned, their faces warped, smiles too wide. Cyran moved on, refusing to linger.

They needed clues, something to lead them to an origin point, a core memory predating the madness. The chained figure's words rang in their head: *Find something that shows him before the grin took root.* If they could locate a significant memory—childhood trauma, an early moment when the Dream Eater first glimpsed this entity—they might piece together how it all began.

At last, one door stood out. Unlike the others, which bore random patterns or twisting marks, this one had a delicate engraving of a simple oval mirror. The etching was crude, as if carved by a trembling hand. Cyran stared at their reflection in it: pale, tense, eyes rimmed red with fear and exhaustion. Behind them, that impossibly thin silhouette hovered, its grin stretching until it seemed to fracture the metal's surface. A ripple ran over the door as if it were liquid. Cyran swallowed hard and reached for the handle.

The door swung open with a soft groan, and they stepped through into a memory that felt different: quieter, more stable. They found themselves in a small, dimly lit bedroom. The air smelled faintly of old dust and candle-wax. A child's bedroom, by the look of it—wooden floors, a narrow bed with a worn quilt, a chest of toys in the corner. A single lantern hung from the ceiling, casting feeble, flickering light.

Cyran's heart clenched. This could be it: a young version of the Dream Eater, before he had earned that terrible name. If they could witness a formative moment, they might glean the truth. They stepped toward the bed. There, under the covers, was a small figure. It took a moment for their eyes to adjust, but then they saw: a boy of perhaps seven or eight, cheeks hollow, eyes open and staring at something in the opposite corner.

Cyran followed his gaze. A mirror stood propped on a wooden stool—an odd feature for a child's bedroom. It was oval, its frame chipped and peeling, the glass tarnished around the edges. At first glance, nothing seemed amiss. Yet the boy's face was drawn, tense, as if he saw something Cyran could not.

From behind them came a faint creak of wood. Cyran whirled, half expecting the grinning entity to materialize. Instead, a door within the memory opened, and a figure entered—a man, tall but stoop-shouldered, dressed in rough work clothes. Perhaps the boy's father. The man's face was weary and pinched, brows knitted. He set a candle on a small table.

"Still awake?" the father asked, voice rough. The boy said nothing. His thin arm emerged from under the quilt, pointing a trembling finger at the mirror.

"Papa," the boy whispered, voice so faint Cyran had to lean in. "There's something in the mirror. It's smiling at me."

Cyran's spine tingled. They dared not move too close, lest they disturb the memory's fragile equilibrium. In dream-walking, direct interference could warp the memory or cause it to disintegrate. Instead, they observed from the perimeter, hidden in a corner of the room where shadows wrapped them like a cloak.

The father sighed, scrubbing a hand over a stubbly chin. "It's just your reflection," he said, exhausted. "We've been over this."

The boy shook his head, tears glistening. "No...no, it's taller than me. It keeps... grinning. It won't go away."

A chill settled in Cyran's lungs. So the child had seen it even then. The entity was present this early, silent and terrible. Was this hallucination the root of the Dream Eater's madness? Or was there truly some presence that latched onto him, feeding off fear?

The father crouched by the bed, voice softening. "We talked about this, remember? It's just a trick of the lantern light. Shadows on the glass. If you keep your eyes closed, it will disappear."

The boy's eyes darted between his father and the mirror. As the father turned, Cyran saw his face flicker strangely, the lantern light casting odd shapes. For a split second, the father's reflection in the mirror elongated, twisting into that impossible grin—just a flicker, gone as soon as noticed. Cyran clutched the side of the toy chest, knuckles whitening. Even as a child, the Dream Eater had been haunted by this vision. No wonder he grew twisted. The very first adults in his life offered no comfort, only denial, leaving him alone with the horror.

The father straightened, impatience creeping into his tone: "Enough of this nonsense. You need sleep." He blew out the candle on the table, leaving only the lantern's dim glow. The memory went slightly darker.

In that dimness, Cyran saw movement in the mirror again. The boy shrank under the covers, whimpering. The reflection in the mirror grew taller, thinner, the grin widening. No words, no sound, just that awful silent smile radiating malevolent glee. Cyran tried to focus on details: the entity's limbs were indistinct, as if made of smoke or shadow. Its eyes were bottomless pits. The grin's edges quivered as though alive.

Then, as if aware of Cyran's presence, the entity in the mirror seemed to shift its head slightly, angling that terrible grin just a fraction toward them. Cyran's heart lurched. This was not just a passive memory—something in here recognized them as an intruder. The grin followed no ordinary rules.

The boy moaned, tears silently streaming. The father, frustrated, stomped out of the room. Alone, the child reached out to the mirror as if compelled. He left the bed, knees knocking, and approached it. Each step revealed how terrified he was, and yet curiosity or some dark magnetism pulled him forward. Cyran wanted to call out, to do something, but they had to remain an observer.

When the boy stood before the mirror, he raised a trembling hand to the glass. For a brief moment, two sets of fingers overlapped: the boy's small, human hand and the entity's elongated, needle-like digits. There was no barrier, no reflection difference. The fingers synced perfectly, as if meeting at the threshold between worlds.

Cyran's stomach churned. This might have been the moment of infection— when the grin first anchored itself to the Dream Eater's mind. A trauma so early, so profound, that the child's psyche had never recovered. Did the child see the grin as a protector, a secret? The chained figure's words returned: *He whispered it to me in the dark.* Perhaps the grin whispered to the boy that night, planting seeds of a worldview that twisted as he matured.

Creak. The floor behind Cyran gave a warning groan. They spun, but nothing was there. Yet the atmosphere changed. The memory's edges began to blur, darken. This scene was not meant to be watched so closely—like a wound forced open, it bled confusion and instability.

The boy in the memory stiffened, his face contorting. The entity's grin widened, as if tasting victory. The boy stumbled back, clutching his head, mouth open in a silent scream. It was as if something inside him was snapping, the fragile sanity of a child confronted with the impossible.

Cyran knew they had to leave before the memory collapsed or the entity trapped them here. They had gotten what they came for: a glimpse of the beginning. The grin had roots in the killer's childhood. It had been with him for a long time, presenting itself as a reflection, a hidden secret. Perhaps the Dream Eater's murders were attempts to free others from illusions, to show them the "truth" the grin had shown him.

But what truth? Cyran had only pieces of the puzzle: a child's terror, a father's dismissal, a grin that persisted in every reflection. The memory began to break apart now, the walls darkening as if soaked in ink. The toy chest melted into a writhing, black mass, and the lantern's light sputtered.

Cyran backed toward the door, but it was gone. Panic licked at their mind. Think, think. They summoned the mental image of the corridor they'd entered from, visualizing the door they'd passed through. Sometimes, forcing a mental focus could restore the path.

With a wrenching sensation, the bedroom flickered. The entity in the mirror twitched, and for a heartbeat, Cyran saw its grin stretch so wide the top of its head nearly peeled back. The boy vanished, the bed rotted away, and the mirror's surface cracked, spilling darkness into the room. Cyran poured all their will into holding onto themselves—Cyran, a Dreamweaver, not part of this mind, an observer.

The darkness thickened, then peeled back. With a gasp, Cyran found themselves in the corridor of mirrors again, stumbling forward as if shoved. They caught themselves on the cold stone wall, breathing hard, sweat trickling down their face. Behind them, each door's reflection still showed that lurking shape, but now it seemed more defined, as if it had grown stronger after revealing its earliest seed to them.

They tried to steady their thoughts, to process what they had learned. The grin was older than the killings, older than even the Dream Eater's adult psyche. It had planted itself in his mind when he was just a frightened child, appearing in reflections, refusing to be explained away. Over the years, it must have guided him, whispering its "truth." Perhaps that truth—that all dreams were illusions to be shattered—led him to murder Dreamweavers who tried to restore those illusions.

Cyran reached for another mental anchor: their own past training. They remembered Aurelius's words: *In every mind, patterns form. Find the pattern and you might find a cure—or at least understand the disease.* The pattern here was reflections. The entity used mirrors, glass, any reflective surface to manifest. Perhaps that was its secret: it needed reflections, gateways, surfaces in which to appear.

Still, what to do with this knowledge? Cyran knew now that healing the killer might be impossible. This wasn't a simple psychological trauma. It felt more like a parasitic presence, embedded so deep that it might have shaped the killer's entire identity. Understanding it might mean acknowledging that the grin could not simply be "removed."

A faint scraping sound trickled down the corridor. Cyran tensed, scanning the gloom. The entity might be more active now. Each success they achieved in uncovering the truth could provoke it. They had to move carefully, glean more insights. The grin's hints—scratch marks on asylum walls, the possibility that it existed beyond just this mind—suggested a threat that transcended the Dream Eater himself.

Cyran pressed on, passing more doors. They would look for anything else that could explain how the grin communicated its message, how it twisted the Dream Eater's psyche. The downward path must continue, deeper into core memories. Maybe they could find a moment when the killer tried to resist or bargain with this entity. Something more tangible.

Behind them, a soft laugh curled through the hall, distorting the mirrors' reflections. Cyran did not turn, but they saw in one mirror a flash of their own face twisting into a grin. They clenched their jaw, refusing to yield. The grin was testing them, wearing down their sense of self.

"I am Cyran," they whispered again, voice taut. "I am here to understand."

They stepped forward, descending ever deeper. The darkness thickened, the air turning cold and stale, as if leading them toward an inner chamber where the killer's adult mind tried to make sense of the grin's truth. If they could find that chamber—some mental library of knowledge, some twisted throne room of the psyche—they might learn the entity's nature. Perhaps they would find a way to loosen its hold, or at least escape before it fully ensnared them.

They tried not to dwell on how the entity had turned to meet their gaze in that memory. If it could see them, truly see them, then this was more than just a nightmare. Something was playing a long, cruel game, and Cyran could feel the rules tightening like a noose.

For now, they gripped their purpose like a lifeline and followed the corridor's descent, each step resonating like a distant heartbeat in a corpse-cold chamber. And behind them, always, the grin lingered, waiting, hungry for the next revelation.

$$4$$

Chapter 4: Hall of Horrors

Cyran pressed onward, descending into the dreamscape's deeper strata. Their surroundings changed subtly at first: the corridor's stone walls developed strange textures, like knotted roots or veins bulging beneath pale skin. The air tasted stale and faintly metallic, as if tinged with blood. The laughter that followed them—soft, distant, yet ever-present—had grown quiet. Now only a muffled whisper remained, so faint it was almost a sensation rather than a sound.

They came to a threshold archway carved from twisted shapes that might have been bones. Beyond it stretched a hallway much longer than any normal architecture would allow—an impossibility characteristic of the dream realm. The space beyond was lit by dim sconces that flickered unevenly, casting monstrous shadows on the walls.

Cyran paused, peering down this hall. The floor looked like old, splintered wood planks, and doors branched off at irregular intervals. Something about the proportions felt wrong—each door too tall, the walls bending inward at odd angles as if leaning down to watch them pass. A memory flickered in Cyran's mind: the first corridor, where they had found dismembered Dreamweavers endlessly rearranging. The chained figure had warned them that they were not the first to delve here, and certainly not the last. Those who failed left imprints behind.

Bracing themselves, they stepped into the hall.

A wet, tearing sound drifted on the stale air. Cyran swallowed. The corridor's end was lost in haze. They approached the first door on their left. It hung ajar, revealing a dim room beyond. Perhaps these rooms might hold fragments of memory—clues to the killer's motivations or the grin's influence. Cyran raised a trembling hand and pushed the door wider.

Inside was a scene that made their stomach clench: the remains of another Dreamweaver, their body spread across a table as if dissected by invisible hands. Limbs twitched and reattached in unnatural configurations—an arm where a leg should be, fingers splayed over a rib-cage, everything in constant, nauseating motion. The victim's face, contorted in agony, bore that same grotesque grin. Whether it was forced by some psychic torment or an imprint of the entity's presence, Cyran couldn't be sure.

They stepped back, bile rising in their throat. It was a reminder that death here would be more than just a mental defeat—it could mean utter psychic obliteration. Cyran forced themselves onward down the hall, not daring to linger on the horrors within these side rooms.

Further along, they heard weeping. The sound was soft and halting. Another door stood slightly open, warm light spilling through. Hesitant but needing to learn more, Cyran nudged it open.

This room looked different: a distorted classroom of some sort, blackboards smeared with red chalk, desks arranged in nonsensical patterns. At the front stood a figure—once human, perhaps—its body flayed open yet still moving, holding chalk in a finger-less hand. On the floor, curled in a corner, something that resembled a Dreamweaver's uniform lay contorted. The figure crying wore a tattered hood, the symbol of the Dreamweaver's guild barely visible beneath dark stains.

Cyran approached carefully. "Hello?" They kept their tone soft. If this was another echo—another psychic fragment—it might provide clues.

The hooded figure jerked at the sound, revealing half of a face devoid of skin. It coughed out words in a strained whisper: "It showed me... the grin... It said all dreams are lies, and I had to unmake them..." The voice hitched, halfway between sob and scream. "I tried. I tried to show him normality. Tried to mend the mind. But it devoured my anchors, turned them inside out."

Cyran's heart sank. Another Dreamweaver who had failed. Their mind had been folded into this horror show. "What is it?" Cyran asked. "Have you learned anything? Anything that can help me escape or understand?"

The figure gurgled, pressing their mangled hands over their face. "No escape. It doesn't want us to understand. It wants us to witness. It wants us to know that all we do is create false comfort. The grin peels away the layers, shows the raw nerves of reality. The Dream Eater accepted this, and so he fed the grin by slaughtering those who would hide truth behind healing."

"Truth?" Cyran whispered. They thought of how Dreamweavers worked—restoring mental balance, easing trauma, helping patients find peace. The grin seemed to view that as deception. Did it consider healing a lie, and suffering the only truth?

"I saw a memory," Cyran said, voice unsteady. "When he was a child, it appeared to him in a mirror. Has it always been with him?"

The figure's single exposed eye rolled, weeping dark tears. "Always... or maybe it found him young. Some minds are fertile soil for such seeds. He tried to tell others. They wouldn't listen. So he listened to it instead."

Cyran pressed their lips tight. They'd confirmed that this entity had long been with the Dream Eater, guiding him to tear apart illusions. But how did that help now?

A scraping sound in the corridor startled them. They glanced back, worried they were being followed. The hallway beyond had grown darker, the sconces dimming as if the dreamscape itself was exhaling its last breath of light. Within the classroom, the desks shifted subtly, legs scraping over the floor. Cyran backed toward the door. Staying here too long would only risk entanglement in these horrors.

Before leaving, Cyran addressed the figure one last time, voice almost gentle: "I'm sorry. I can't help you." The figure only sobbed and continued muttering nonsense about illusions and truths.

Cyran slipped back into the corridor, sweat trickling down their spine. They had more confirmation now: the grin's philosophy—or whatever this entity represented—was anathema to Dreamweavers. It thrived on unveiling horrors rather than healing minds. If the Dream Eater became a murderer, perhaps he believed he was doing the world a favor by shattering comforting lies. Or maybe the grin forced him to see everyone's inner nightmares and commanded him to set them free by destroying them.

The corridor stretched on. The laughter they had heard before returned in tiny spurts. Another door, another peek inside, revealed yet more carnage—limbs of Dreamweavers suspended like puppets on iron hooks, each with that unnatural grin. Cyran slammed that door shut, horrified.

They marched forward, refusing to be paralyzed by fear. They needed something more useful—some direct confrontation or fragment where the Dream Eater's voice might explain himself more coherently. Thus far, everything was chaos and hints. If the grin's logic was that suffering was truth, then perhaps understanding that logic would offer a way out: by demonstrating they understood, maybe Cyran could slip free of the entity's influence.

Their footsteps on the warped planks grew heavier, as though gravity had intensified. The corridor seemed to react to their resolve, twisting, the end receding. Cyran thought of the tools they had as a Dreamweaver—mental constructs to anchor and shape the dream. They tried one now: imagining a door at the end of the hallway that would lead them somewhere revealing, a "safe room" of sorts. If they could impose their will, they might steer the dream.

Closing their eyes, Cyran pictured a heavy oak door at the corridor's terminus, its surface carved with runes of clarity and healing. They focused, exerting quiet pressure on the dream's fabric. When they opened their eyes, the corridor flickered, wood panels shifting. At the far distance, just barely visible through the gloom, they thought they saw a door that hadn't been there a moment before.

A triumphant spark lit Cyran's chest. Dreamweavers could influence the mental landscape, even if it was dangerous. They pushed forward, half running now, ignoring the doors that branched off to horrors. The laughter rose behind them, as if offended by this attempt at control.

The corridor protested: doors slammed open and shut on their own, ink-dark fluid seeped through cracks in the floor, and dismembered hands crawled along the walls, each finger capped with a tiny grin. Cyran gritted their teeth, refusing to be deterred.

As they neared the oak door, a thunderous crack shook the world. A shadowy form darted across their path, all angles and long limbs, trailing an echo of mirthless laughter. Cyran stumbled, nearly falling. Their heart hammered. They caught a glimpse of its face—just a blur, but the grin was unmistakable.

The grin wouldn't let them go. Yet they had to try. With a surge of will, Cyran lunged for the oak door's handle and pulled it open. Beyond lay a descending spiral staircase carved into stone, lit by faint torches. They didn't hesitate; they plunged into the stairwell, letting the door swing shut behind them.

The laughter muffled. On the staircase, a new atmosphere took hold: heavy silence, broken only by their rasping breath. The stairs spiraled downward, promising deeper layers of the Dream Eater's psyche. Deeper memories, maybe. Or the killer's internal "throne room" where the grin's presence was strongest. If Cyran wanted understanding—if they wanted any hope of leaving this mind intact—they had to confront the core.

They descended carefully, each footstep echoing. The stone walls were moist with condensation, and roots poked through, suggesting they were going underground—or deeper into psychic bedrock. With each step, Cyran repeated their mantra: "I am Cyran. I am an observer. I am here to understand." Over and over, like a talisman against the grin's corrosive presence.

At last, the staircase ended at a small landing. Before them was a heavy iron door, unadorned, with no lock. A thin line of flickering light shone beneath it. Cyran placed their ear close, listening. A voice drifted through—ragged, disjointed words. Could it be the Dream Eater himself, or another echo?

They gripped the handle, steeling themselves. The horrors behind them had been warnings, attempts to scare them off or break their resolve. Now they would press on, deeper still, searching for the truth. It wouldn't be easy. They had seen how the grin delighted in torment and distortion. But maybe, somewhere behind that door, there would be a sliver of coherence—a clue to the grin's nature, how it took root, and what it intended outside this mind.

Cyran inhaled and pushed the door open, stepping once more into uncertainty, holding their identity and purpose like a fragile flame against an endless dark.

5

Chapter 5: Twisted Memories

The iron door swung inward with a sullen groan, and Cyran stepped into a long, low chamber that felt like the belly of some ancient beast. The ceiling sagged in warped arches overhead, and the floor was uneven, littered with broken glass, shattered porcelain masks, and torn scraps of old letters. A few guttering candles—hardly more than lumps of wax—provided feeble light. Their flames were strange colors: bruised purples, sickly greens, casting wavering shadows on the stone walls.

No laughter greeted them here, no immediate sign of the grin. Yet Cyran sensed it lingering at the edges, just out of sight. The silence in this room felt deliberate, expectant. They moved forward, careful not to cut themselves on the shards beneath their boots. The fragments crunched underfoot, their sound echoing oddly.

A voice drifted through the dimness, uneven and low, like someone muttering beneath blankets. Cyran stepped gingerly around a toppled chair and found the source: a figure crouched near a far corner, half hidden by a collapsed bookshelf. At first glance, it looked almost normal—an adult man dressed in a drab, threadbare coat. His back was turned, shoulders hunched. He scratched at the floor with broken fingernails, mumbling words that danced in and out of coherence.

Cyran's heart quickened. This might be a direct manifestation of the Dream

Eater himself—an avatar of the killer's conscious mind, or at least a significant fragment. If so, maybe here they could get answers without the grin's constant interference. Cyran approached slowly, making sure their voice was calm and low.

"Hello?" they said softly, standing a few paces away. "Can you hear me?"

The figure tensed. His hands froze, claws hovering over the shards. After a moment, he turned his head slightly, revealing a profile that was gaunt and hollow-cheeked. His eyes, sunken deep, flickered with watery light. He looked neither mad nor calm—just weary, as if he'd been locked in this place too long.

"You came," he muttered, voice slurred as if drunk. "Another Dreamweaver, yes?"

Cyran dipped their head. "I'm here to understand what happened to you." They tried not to let fear or revulsion slip into their tone.

The man's lips twitched. "You want to understand. They all want to understand. They come in with their theories, their gentle voices, their illusions of healing." He plucked a piece of porcelain off the floor and turned it over in his fingers. It was part of a mask's cheek, painted with a fragment of a grin. "But you cannot heal what is... correct." He said that last word with reverence, as if speaking a sacred truth. "The others thought I was mad. Maybe I am. But madness is a door. Through it, you see clearly."

Cyran's throat tightened. "See what?"

He offered a hollow smile that did not fully reach his eyes. "The grin. The thing behind the world's facade. Do you know what dreams are, Dreamweaver? They're painted screens, hiding uglier truths. You ease trauma, mend minds, restore order—fine brushstrokes over raw chaos." He closed his eyes and sighed. "The grin doesn't lie. It shows what lies beneath all those smiles we wear."

Cyran steadied themselves. The man spoke as if influenced directly by that entity. "You mean the entity showed you something. A vision? Some knowledge that made you... turn on others."

"Turn on others?" He shrugged. "I freed them. Their dreams lied to them, and the grin showed me that the only way to truly see is to tear the dream apart, to show them the raw wound beneath the bandage. I tried to help the

Dreamweavers see, too, but they screamed and died." He chuckled, a sound without humor. "Not my fault. They didn't want the truth."

A heavy silence followed. Cyran gritted their teeth. This was dangerous ground. Showing anger or fear might feed the mind's hostility. They must remain calm, analytical.

"You met the grin as a child," Cyran said, probing gently. "In a mirror. It frightened you then."

The man's eyes went distant, unfocused. "Yes, a child. I was so small. I tried to tell them—my father, anyone—what I saw. They laughed or brushed it aside. I thought I was cursed." He paused, then tapped his temple. "But the grin... it taught me. Over time, I understood it was no curse. It was an unveiling. The world's masks are fragile. You, Dreamweavers, you patch those masks, never asking if it's better to see the underlying rot."

Cyran took a step closer, ignoring the way the man's words twisted their stomach. "The grin—do you know what it is? Is it part of you or something else entirely?"

A flicker of uncertainty crossed the man's face. He cast his gaze down. "Part of me? Maybe. It came from outside, or maybe it was always inside. Does the difference matter?" He set the porcelain shard down. "It lives in reflections, in the cracks of perception. It can stretch beyond my mind, I think. Maybe it finds fertile ground in others, too." A half-smile pulled at his lips. "Haven't you felt it? The tug at the corners of your vision, the sense it's behind you, even now?"

Cyran suppressed a shudder. They had felt it: the grin lurking in mirrors, looming in reflections. "What does it want?"

The man tilted his head, as if puzzled by the question. "Wants? Who can say? To it, our suffering and our revelations are just... music. It laughs because it can. It shows the truth because that is its nature." He met Cyran's eyes at last, and in that gaze, Cyran saw a broken soul. "You think it evil? Maybe it's indifferent. Or maybe, just maybe, it hates illusions as much as you hate horrors."

Cyran's mind spun. So the grin was a force of some sort, feeding on despair or clarity, depending on one's perspective. If it existed beyond this mind, if it could appear in the waking world, what did that mean? The Department wanted a diagnosis—some explanation for the Dream Eater's madness. Cyran was realizing that the Dream Eater was merely the grin's instrument, or its disciple. Killing Dreamweavers might have been his twisted attempt to remove those who preserved comforting lies. He had tried to show the world what he saw, one victim at a time.

"How do I leave?" Cyran asked quietly. "I've learned something of what you've shown me. But if I stay here, I'll end up like the others."

The man closed his eyes again. "Leave?" His voice lowered, thoughtful. "If you truly want to leave, you must either accept the grin's vision or reject it utterly. Understanding alone is dangerous—like holding a blade by its edge." He paused as if listening to distant whispers. "You must make a choice: do you embrace what the grin reveals, or do you deny it and hold onto the comfort of your Dreamweaver illusions?"

Cyran frowned. Was that a riddle or a real key to escape? Their entire craft was about finding balance, healing psychic wounds. The grin's philosophy was an affront to everything Cyran believed in. They couldn't embrace it. But perhaps acknowledging its existence and maintaining faith in their own purpose could form a stable path out.

The man seemed to sense Cyran's turmoil. "You hesitate. Wise. The grin abhors absolute ignorance, but it also scorns shallow compromise. If you try to run from here without internalizing something you've seen... I doubt it will let you go unscathed."

Cyran's heart sank. They would have to carry some of this truth back. Not fully believing it, but recognizing it, might keep the grin at bay. Perhaps the Department's leaders were right: just understanding that this presence might be beyond mere trauma was the key. Maybe once Cyran returned, they could warn the outside world, or at least record what they saw. But would that spread the grin's influence further?

Before they could speak again, a low rumble shook the chamber. The bookshelf behind the man collapsed into ash. He rose to his feet, swaying, as the shards on the floor melted into black sludge. The candles sputtered, their flames turning red. The grin's influence stirred, restless.

The man looked around, alarmed. "It knows you've come far. It's testing your resolve. If you want to confront it, or at least face it on your terms, you must go deeper." He pointed to a new opening in the far wall—a ragged hole that had not been there a moment before. "Through there lies another layer. A place where I once tried to reason with it. You might find the truth you seek."

Cyran followed his gesture. The hole gaped like a wound in the stone, dripping some viscous fluid. Horrifying, but they had come this far. Perhaps facing the grin more directly could offer a final piece of the puzzle.

Cyran turned back to the man. "Will you come with me?"

The killer shook his head, sadness carving lines on his hollow face. "I am part of this now. Bound to it. Even if I wanted to leave, I doubt I could. The grin and I have danced too long." He gave a bitter smile. "Go. Do what you came to do. Just remember: your mind is your own—but the grin will always watch, should you falter."

A whisper of gratitude died unspoken on Cyran's lips. There was no saving this man; he was too deeply enmeshed in the grin's logic. Still, he had provided guidance. With a nod, Cyran turned and approached the hole. The stone around it seemed to pulsate, the fluid trickling down in thick rivulets. The smell of damp earth and coppery blood intensified.

A voice, distant and mocking, drifted through the opening. It sounded like laughter layered over screams. Cyran's chest tightened, but there was no turning back now. They had to see this through—learn the grin's final secret or at least force a confrontation that might allow them to exit this hellish mind intact.

They stepped through, and the hole sealed behind them with a moist squelch, leaving the killer's fragment alone in the chamber. As Cyran pressed forward, the temperature dropped, and the walls of this new passage quivered as if alive. Everything here would be a test of will. The grin would try to break them or convert them. Cyran had to hold on to their identity, their purpose as a healer, and their understanding that not all illusions are lies—some are kindnesses, necessary for sanity.

Ahead, a flicker of light and the echo of that infernal laughter guided them deeper. The encounter with the Dream Eater's fragment had offered partial truths. Now, perhaps, Cyran would see the grin itself, or at least what passed for its heart. And then they could decide what to believe and what to reject. How to maintain their own self-hood in the face of something that seemed to transcend mere nightmares.

Cyran inhaled, steadying their trembling limbs, and marched into the darkness, determined to face the entity and survive.

6

Chapter 6: The Maze of Teeth

The walls around Cyran convulsed in slow, rhythmic spasms, their surfaces slick and organic, as though the architecture of the Dream Eater's mind had given way to living tissue. The air was heavier here, thick with the scent of decay and old secrets unearthed. There were no proper corridors now—only twisting passages that writhed and twisted like intestinal tracts. Every so often, a muffled laugh would pulse through the darkness, making the walls contract, hinting that the grin was close by, enjoying their plight.

Cyran moved forward step by careful step. The ground felt spongy underfoot, and as they reached out to steady themselves against the quivering tunnel sides, they realized the surface was studded with small, irregular shapes. At first, Cyran thought them to be jagged stones or bits of bone. Leaning closer, they recognized their shape—teeth. Hundreds of crooked teeth, embedded in walls of fleshy texture, as if the hallway were a colossal mouth or a vast digestive tract lined with incisors. The Maze of Teeth—Cyran recalled the earlier vision of a hallway like this—an omen of what awaited at the center.

A shiver coursed through them. They could not afford fear. Fear would feed the grin, loosen their grasp on identity. Instead, they repeated their anchor mantra: "I am Cyran. I am a Dreamweaver, here to understand." Their voice came back hollow and absorbed by the living darkness.

After several turns—no clear direction but forward—a shadow flickered at the periphery of Cyran's vision. They whirled, expecting an ambush. Instead, the flicker became a murky silhouette drifting ahead, barely visible in the half-light. No details showed: just a long-limbed shape gliding silently around a bend. Cyran's heart pounded. They followed, cautiously, knowing they had to confront the entity or risk wandering these twisting guts forever.

As they turned the corner, they found a broader space—a chamber with a domed ceiling of interlocking fangs. Pale membranes stretched between tooth-like growths, filtering a dim, unnatural light. In the center of this macabre cathedral stood a figure cloaked in shadow. Tall and impossibly thin, it was shaped vaguely like a human but stretched too long, with limbs that tapered into points. The grin on its face glowed faintly, like a crescent moon over a black sea. Its eyes were featureless voids, yet Cyran felt its gaze land on them like a tangible weight.

The entity neither moved nor spoke. It simply stood, grinning. Cyran's breath caught. This was the closest they had come to it without the buffer of illusions. Here, in the core of the Dream Eater's psyche, the grin had physical form—if "physical" was the right word. A nightmare given shape, waiting.

They forced themselves to speak. "I know what you are," Cyran said, voice trembling but determined. "Or at least, I know what you represent. You show the truth beneath illusions. You've been with him since childhood, haven't you? Twisting his understanding, making him believe that all comfort is a lie."

No response. The grin's mouth curved wider, its shape shifting subtly as if amused. Cyran felt an invisible pressure in the air, like standing too close to a powerful electric field.

"Why?" Cyran pressed on. "Why him? Why anyone? Are you a parasite? A manifestation of trauma? Or do you come from somewhere else entirely?"

A sound that might have been laughter pulsed through the chamber, making the teeth in the dome clatter softly. Cyran realized the entity would not simply explain itself—it thrived on ambiguity. They recalled what the Dream Eater's fragment had said: *You must either accept the grin's vision or reject it utterly.*

But what did acceptance or rejection mean here?

Cyran centered themselves. They were a Dreamweaver, trained to handle twisted psyches. Normally, healing involved gently guiding the patient toward understanding and catharsis. But this was different. The grin did not seem like a wounded fragment that could be healed. It was a force, almost elemental, that took delight in stripping away all comfort.

Yet Cyran also knew that illusions—dreams—were not mere lies. They could be kindness, solace, a bridge to recovery. Not all truths needed to be raw and brutal. People needed hope. If the grin's philosophy was that all illusions must be torn down, Cyran would stand against it. Not by denying that horrors exist, but by asserting that human beings can choose compassion and healing even in the face of them.

They spoke slowly, voice echoing among the tooth-lined walls: "You show horrors. Fine. Horrors exist. Pain and madness are part of the human mind. But so is resilience. So is the capacity to dream and heal. Dreamweavers don't just hide the truth—we help people live with it. If that means comforting illusions, sometimes that's what's needed. Healing is not always a lie—it can be a gentle truth, a truth that says we can endure and improve."

The grin's silent face twitched. Its head tilted unnaturally, as if listening intently. Cyran's chest tightened. They were pushing back, asserting their role as a healer. The grin might lash out now. But Cyran had no weapon except conviction and understanding.

"I see you, grin," Cyran said, tears pricking their eyes. "I see that you're a force that thrives on despair and brutality, revealing what people fear most. You want me to submit, to believe your vision is the only one. But I refuse. I know horrors exist—and I choose to help people cope, not force them into insanity."

The chamber darkened. The candle-like glow dimmed. The grin's silence was a terrifying reproach. Cyran's vision swam, and for a moment, they thought they saw other faces flickering in the darkness: Dreamweavers who had failed, the Dream Eater's victims, all grinning hopelessly. The grin wanted to show that resistance was futile.

Cyran clenched their jaw. They wouldn't yield. They reached into their mental toolkit and summoned every protective technique they knew: visu alizing a sphere of calm light around themselves, remembering their name and purpose, recalling a time they had helped a patient recover from trauma. The memory came to them: a young woman who had lost her family, whose nightmares Cyran had soothed. They had guided her through images of love, of gentle reassurances, helping her accept her loss without succumbing to despair. That wasn't lying—it was healing.

With that memory glowing in their mind, Cyran stepped toward the grin, just one pace. It loomed taller, but they did not falter.

"You may exist," Cyran said softly, voice steadying. "You may even extend beyond this mind. Maybe I'll see you again in reflections in the waking world. But I will never stop believing in the value of healing. I acknowledge that suffering is real, but so is hope."

For a long, excruciating moment, nothing happened. The grin's face remained fixed, that crescent mouth stretching beyond what should be anatomically possible. The silence was absolute.

Then, a subtle shift: the grin's head bobbed, almost like a nod, or was it a trick of the flickering light? The pressure in the chamber eased a fraction. Cyran felt their lungs fill more easily. Had the entity accepted their stance, or was it simply amused by this defiance?

Without a word, the grin began to recede into the darkness, its shape elongating until it was just a faint silhouette etched against the far wall. It left behind a resonance, a lingering presence that seemed to say: *You have seen me, and you carry that knowledge now.* There was no triumphant fanfare, no confirmation that Cyran's stance was correct. The grin remained as enigmatic as ever. But it was retreating. That might be the closest thing to a victory possible here.

Cyran stood alone, heart pounding. Was that the test? They had neither embraced the grin's philosophy nor denied the existence of horror. Instead, they acknowledged suffering but championed healing. Perhaps this nuanced stance was enough. Perhaps it granted them permission to leave this nightmare and return to their body.

The chamber quivered, and a line of light appeared at one side—a slit in the fleshy wall. Cyran approached it, and as they drew near, it widened, becoming a doorway outlined in sickly light. They stepped through, hoping it would lead them up and out of the Dream Eater's psyche. The laughter behind them faded to a distant echo. The teeth in the walls rattled softly, like the closing notes of a horrid symphony.

As they passed through the threshold, Cyran felt a rushing sensation, as if being pulled upward by invisible currents. The darkness around them frayed into static, then blurred into pale washes of color. Their limbs went numb. The stale smell vanished, replaced by sterile antiseptic. Voices buzzed at the edge of hearing—urgent, worried voices.

With a gasp, Cyran opened their eyes to find themselves back in the sedation chamber. The technicians hovered over them. They peeled electrodes from Cyran's temples. The silver-haired department head stood behind glass, observing, her lips a thin line of expectation.

Cyran's body shook with residual terror and awe. They had made it out, though their mind still swirled with images of grinning faces and impossible corridors of teeth. They knew better now: the Dream Eater's madness was not just trauma—it was an encounter with something deeper, something that might touch others. Something that not even the waking world's walls could fully contain.

But they had survived, and in surviving, they carried a message the outside world might never truly grasp. They had to try and explain. They had to let the Department know what lurked inside that mind. Not that it would be easy. They might dismiss it as metaphor, or they might fear that Cyran was infected by this grin. Perhaps they were, in some subtle way. The mirror's reflection would always be suspect now.

As the guards unstrapped them, Cyran met the department head's gaze through the observation window. They managed a trembling nod. The head narrowed her eyes, surprised. They had expected a failure, a corpse. Instead, they had their survivor. Their witness.

Cyran closed their eyes briefly, remembering the grin's final silent exchange. They understood something crucial: The grin had not been defeated—perhaps it could never be—but it had acknowledged them. And they had returned to tell the tale, carrying both horror and hope intertwined.

It would have to be enough.

7

Chapter 7 (Epilogue): Echoes in the Glass

In the weeks following the mission, the facility settles into a subdued routine. Outside, autumn deepens, painting the sky in quieter hues of gray and gold. Inside, no one mentions the Dream Eater by name unless required by protocol. The Department's staff move with measured calm, as though unwilling to disturb the fragile peace that has fallen since Cyran survived where so many others perished.

Cyran finds themselves back in a small, private office. After multiple assessments and careful observation, their status as a Dreamweaver is reinstated. There's no fanfare, just a sealed envelope with a renewed identification card slipped under their door one morning. The card's holographic eye stares impassively, a silent reminder of the system they serve and the ordeal they endured.

They resume work gradually, taking on low-level trauma cases—simple nightmares, minor anxieties. Patients greet Cyran with hopeful faces, never knowing the horrors their healer has faced. Cyran does their job quietly, using the techniques honed through pain and fear. They guide patients through twisted memories, helping them find calm, each small success reassuring that their role matters.

But outside the therapy rooms, whispers linger. A few staff members still eye Cyran with a strange mixture of respect and unease. Survivors of the

Department's earlier attempts at understanding the Dream Eater's psyche pass in the corridors, giving them polite nods. None of them speak of the grin or the entity Cyran glimpsed deep in that monstrous mindscape, yet the absence of such talk feels deliberate, as if everyone agreed not to tug too hard at the edges of what they almost understand.

In spare moments, Cyran wanders the building's quiet corners. There's a janitorial closet near the old observation wing, its door always kept locked. A rumor says that inside, faint scratch marks mar the walls—like someone tried to carve out a grin that would not fade. Cyran never sees these marks personally, but the rumor suffices. It's proof that the past cannot be erased with silence.

Occasionally, Cyran catches their own reflection in a window or a polished floor panel. Now and then, the light bends strangely, a trick of perception making shadows seem a fraction taller, a grin a sliver too wide. Each time, Cyran blinks, and reality snaps back to normal. They can't be sure if it's just a lingering paranoia or if some remnant of that entity still brushes against the world's edges.

They never doubt what they accomplished, though. Entering the Dream Eater's mind was not pointless. From that descent into horror, Cyran carried out insight—awareness that not all nightmares can be neatly cured, that some terrors defy easy classification. That knowledge has made them a better Dreamweaver. Patients who once would have terrified them are now approached with tempered courage. Cyran knows how to anchor themselves and guide others through impossible darkness.

As for the entity, the grin, the question of its true nature remains unanswered. Cyran stands one evening by a reinforced window overlooking the courtyard. Guards patrol below. In the distance, autumn leaves swirl, and the sky fades into an uncertain dusk. If the grin still exists somewhere—lurking in reflections, biding its time—Cyran understands now they cannot destroy it with certainty. But they can face it, and that matters. The Dream Eater's rampage might never be fully explained, but the attempt to understand it, to confront the horrors behind it, has changed the Dreamweavers who remain.

Before heading home, Cyran presses a palm against the cool glass. Their reflection meets their gaze: tired eyes, determined set of jaw. No impossible grin warps those features now. Perhaps the entity watches from afar, amused or frustrated by the resilience it inadvertently nurtured. Or perhaps it's gone, drifting back into the mental shadows that spawned it.

Cyran steps away, leaving the reflection behind. The building's corridors lead them back to a world where healing is still possible, where dreams and nightmares mingle but do not wholly define one's fate. The mystery is not resolved, but it does not invalidate what came before. Each patient Cyran helps, each quiet victory, reaffirms that their journey mattered.

And if, one day, a distant laugh or a warping shadow in the corner of a mirror suggests that the grin has returned, Cyran—and the others who learned from this ordeal—will be ready.